Frank Smith Brittain

Oscar and Esther

And other poems

Frank Smith Brittain

Oscar and Esther
And other poems

ISBN/EAN: 9783337207045

Printed in Europe, USA, Canada, Australia, Japan

Cover: Foto ©Andreas Hilbeck / pixelio.de

More available books at **www.hansebooks.com**

OSCAR AND ESTHER,

AND OTHER POEMS.

OSCAR AND ESTHER,

AND OTHER POEMS.

BY

FRANK SMITH BRITTAIN.

LONDON :

WYMAN & SONS, GREAT QUEEN STREET,

LINCOLN'S-INN FIELDS, W.C.

1883.

TO

MY SISTER,

IN TESTIMONY OF MY LOVE, AND BELIEF IN HERS,

I Dedicate

THE FOLLOWING METRICAL TRIFLES,

SEEKING THUS TO GAIN FOR THEM

AN EXTRINSIC VALUE.

233, BRISTOL STREET, BIRMINGHAM,
June, 1883.

CONTENTS.

	PAGE
Oscar and Esther	1
A Dream	30
Musings	40
Flowing, smiling, e'er beguiling	43
I love to dream	45
To the Muse	48
Art Thou in the Desert?	55
A Grave Scene	57
On a Faded Leaf	59
My True Love is Dead!	61
A Motherless Maid...	63
Flush, Cheek and Brow	67
When Passion doth my Temples heat ...	71
My Soul, Great God	73

viii CONTENTS.

	PAGE
To Death	75
We did not kiss	77
I saw last Night	80
One so Dark and One so Fair	82
Most Lovely Girl	85
The Swallows	87
Little Birdie, why so Gay?	89
Faded Bunch of Violets	91
Sleep on, Sweet Love	94
To my Mother on her Jubilee	96
I sorrow for Thee this Morn	99
Father Christmas	102
Since Thou art all my own, Fairy ...	104
Her Look when last	106
All will yet come right	108

OSCAR AND ESTHER.

Of Love I sing ! and crave a voice
   Whose accents round the world might ring
Melodious, soft and clear, more choice
   Than lark's when on the sun-lit wing.
Each human heart should pity feel,
E'en were the tend'rest hard as steel.

Fair maidens with a maid should weep,
   And own a kindred hope and fear,
Till, lost in fancies strange as deep,
   Should flow the sympathetic tear.
Creations of the fervid mind
Should forms and habitations find.

*   *   *   *   *

B

On rocky summit, wild and weird,
  Around its base a moaning wood,
A gloomy castle rests, revered
  As home of brave men and of good ;
In times of old it oft had been
The witness of a martial scene.

Its deep recesses too have heard,
  In twilight's soft and deep'ning shades,
Bold warriors breathe the tender word,
  To win the hearts of comely maids ;
Its ancient arches loud have rung
In echo to the festive song.

A youth stept forth, of noble mien,
  Out from the keep, and dash'd the dew
From off the grass, as from the scene
  With quickening steps of rage he flew ;
His eyes were bright, his cheeks were red,
Alternate with the white of dread.

The waking sun had kiss'd the hills,
   The distant lake was all aglow,
Sparkling in many thousand rills
   That o'er its murm'ring wavelets flow ;
But noted not by him who flew,
And dash'd from off the grass the dew.

Nought of this lovely scene he sees,
   For, smiling sadly far away,
A something, flitting as he flees,
   Seems to allure him on his way,—
A face so sad, almost too fair
To mingle with the mortal air.

A lovely hand that calls for aid
   Impatiently doth beckon on :
Forwards he press'd ; but once he stay'd ;—
   It broke the spell ; his Love was gone ;—
The trance was ended ; sense again
Recall'd him to a life of pain :

For, surging thro' his every limb,
　The mad blood rush'd in awful haste,
His teeth were clench'd, his eyes were dim,
　As 'cross his brain the hot thoughts chased.
Ah ! death were nought to him, I trow,
With fiery eye and wrinkled brow—

Yea, death were heaven, compared with grief
　That rends that heart with sorrow full,
And hell almost would bring relief
　If recollection it could dull;
But brave is he, and all life's day
Will front the gloom that crowds its way,

Keeping stern courage still to bear
　Until Oblivion's waves shall sweep
And set the pris'ner free from care,
　Sinking the carcass in the deep,
Granting the soul its power to flee,
And wake to its infinity.

'Tis hard to die.   I trow, to live
  Is sterner still.   Call them not brave
Who fling away their lives and give
  The conflict up; to seek the grave.
A cur but howls and takes to flight;
A babe but shrinks from dark of night.

Yet e'en the bravest heart must quail,
  When sorely tried and sear'd with care,
Feel it almost a joy to fail,
  A double death to do and dare,
As each day's battle sterner grows,
And rends its depths with wilder throes.

The spell-bound youth from out his breast
  A lock of golden hair now drew,
His lips against it gently press'd,
  And on the winds a blessing threw
To her with that sad face so fair,
That mingled with the morning air,—

And, as he gazed upon the tress,
   A tear crept in his large dark eye;
He knew there could not be redress,
   For grief like his would blush to die.
A youth so full of fervent life,
He learnt—how far too soon!—'tis rife

With biting words and cruel deeds,
   And discontentments born of care,
Its brightness dull, its flowers but weeds,
   Its trust a half-disguised despair—
A dark unfathomable sea,
Whose breakers roar unceasingly.

Oh! saddest, saddest day, when first
   The young life, blushing in its morn,
With loving hope, yearning to burst
   Into the future yet unborn,
Is clutchèd by the hand of Fate,
Which stifles hope with ruthless hate.

Oh ! cruel hour as black as night,
  Surrounded with the light of day,
For ever foremost to the sight
  Of times that long have pass'd away,
When first, deep in the trusting heart,
Sad disappointment hurl'd her dart.

Alone it stands, and roughly wakes
  The tender soul to hate and dread,
The signal of a grief that takes
  The joy and buoyancy of tread
From our lone walk—hence roads are bare,
Sharp points th' unguarded feet will tear.

The spell has gone, we know we live—
  But, like a fruit-tree nipp'd with frost,
Back the first freshness nought can give.
  The lesson's learnt ; but dire's the cost,
For autumn's harvesting must show,
The plant could not efface the blow—

Say some brain-addled fools, 'tis best,
    Ere yet the shoot is strong with life,
Or, while with tender blossom dress'd,
    To strip it with chill winter's knife—
As well toss out a child to swim,
Deform'd or maim'd in every limb.

Ah me, the morn too soon will break !
    The truth too soon will rend the veil,
And from the choicest blossom take
    The bloom of life, and leave it pale
With burning thought, that trembling peers
In the dark gloom of coming years.

At least the youth, whose lips had press'd
    The lock of hair of golden hue,
Felt in the caverns of his breast
    The stormy voyage he'd learn'd to rue—
But causes make our anger glow,
We feel the shaft, but curse the bow.

And had he cause to curse the hand
   Which mark'd the course the arrow took,
Shatt'ring the wondrous magic wand
   That erst made all propitious look?
Opinions vary,—hear my tale,
Then grant he had true cause to wail.

ᴧ

Few leagues (not more), of gentlest heart,
   Sweet Esther lived. A joyous maid,
With beaming eyes that knew not art,
   With locks so bright they cast a shade
Upon the sun; with lips so red—
Oh, for the kisses they could shed!

Her brow was soft and clear as snow,
   Her laugh so thrilling and so gay,
Heard on the breeze to ebb and flow,
   Like song from thrush in smiling May;
Her face the same, with heav'nly gleam,
That Oscar saw in morning dream.

And these had learn'd to love so young—
    With love and faith so strong and true?
Venus, alas! her garb had flung;
    What else beside could then ensue?
The force of will all passions bends,
Save Love, which strongest will transcends.

By reason's light Love is not led,
    Nor by the feeble will controll'd—
'Tis subject to the voice which said,
    Let worlds in empty space be roll'd;
From Him it came, to Him returns;
For Him it cools, for Him it burns.

But what is Love?   No empty sound
    That rolls along the carnal tongue,—
Not smiling face or ankles round,
    Not light'ning eyes or sighs drawn long;
Not kisses on the ruby lip,
Nor oath, as sparkling wine we sip.

And yet Love ripples on the tongue,
  And adds new beauty to the singer ;
And in a sigh you catch its song,
  And on the lips it loves to linger ;
And breathes forth in the sacred vow,
From souls who at her altar bow.

To Esther's early days were known
  Rich blessings of maternal love.
That parent spirit since had flown,
  Tired of the strife, and, like the dove
Which left the Ark, her weary breast
Sought fairer realms—unbroken rest.

What countless numbers justly claim
  The appellation " Mother dear ! "
They who have won the holy name
  Which quickest starts the filial tear.
A sainted mother never dies,
Perennial her precepts rise.

Too often, like a bell, not heard
    Till struck, then what a mighty peal
There comes from each remember'd word
    Of love ! From out the past we steal
Our joys, and gladly call to mind
The life so gentle and resign'd.

Yea, they live in nobler sense
    Than in a frame of massive gold ;
There is within the mind, from whence
    We draw, with Recollection's mould,
A breathing portrait, true to life,
Of loving mother, noble wife !

Oh, heaven-born memory ! we weave
    Thee garlands of immortal flowers,
Eternity shall not bereave
    Thee of our gifts, but heap new dowers—
A monument above thine head,
Round which bright angel feet shall tread.

Sweet recollections that can call
    The hallow'd form again to view—
The voice that still can us enthrall,
    Whose accents ever rang so true—
Those eyes still smile, we feel the hand
That's pass'd into the Father Land.

Oscar and Esther loved.   Too late
    Their elders read the truth, to crush
Within their souls the joy elate
    Of deep'ning love.   They felt the rush
Of new delights, new hopes, as age
Disclosed its daily length'ning page.

Their love no mortal might could stay;
    But mortal might can check the means
Whereby Love lights and cheers our way,
    And lends enchantment to its scenes—
The foaming cup of bliss can break,
Or from our paths the roses take.

Ah, sad uncertainties of life ;
　　'Tis well we do not always stay
To recollect how sadly rife
　　We are with death and quick decay ;
That a brief instant may efface
The picture late so full of grace.

But yesterday, on Fancy's wing,
　　Thy future how serene and bright !
To-day it lends the double sting
　　That doth thine aching soul affright.
Man but soars high to fall again,
As Life and Death alternate reign.

＊　　　　＊　　　　＊　　　　＊

And tell of her, thy maiden dear,
　　Has she received a wound, so fair ?—
Have her sweet eyes to shed a tear ?
　　Has her kind heart to own a care ?
No wonder, then, thou hast, I trow,
A fiery eye and wrinkled brow.

O that Ambition's noblest aim
   Were to see loving ones unite ;
Their hopes alike, their souls one flame,
   A flame of love in living light !
Oh ! what is wealth, compared to this,
But dross, at which dark hell might hiss ?

Yet sad it is that dross can part
   Two loving souls, and cast a gloom
That gathers round the trusting heart,
   And speeds it to the silent tomb.
The tomb ! Then wealth, if thou hadst all,
Could only make a richer pall.

*   *   *   *   *

Oscar, thy own true love I view'd
   As in dark night she lonely wandered,
In robe of pearly white, imbued
   With saintly beauty ; and I pondered
How God must surely grant the prayer
Of one so pure and passing fair.

When softly on the midnight air
Her solemn voice, in accents sweet,
Broke forth.   Nor wanting strength, for care
Makes resolute the will, and fleet
The foot, when rises into view
The throne where none in vain can sue.

Myself I all forgot, and gazed
In admiration mute, but true—
As on the night her beauty blazed,
And as her soul in fervour threw
Its burthen'd cares to worlds on high,
Far, far beyond the starlit sky.

An angel she appear'd ! and bared
Her heart to the immortal sight ;
For that is prayer !   If thou hadst heard,
Thou would'st have said its very might,
Forth bursting from this mortal tomb,
A world might save from righteous doom.

And once the pale moon gently sent
   Her mild effulgence o'er her face,
Where in sweet unison were blent
   The earthly form and heavenly grace.
See, glist'ring on that deep blue eye
The heavy tears of sorrow lie.

I pray thee take thy watch to-night,
   And there, ensconced in leafy bower,
She may appear to bless thy sight,
   Disconsolate, in midnight's hour ;
In accents that thou deemest meet,
Thou may'st thy lovely lady greet.

     *   *   *   *   *

The night on raven wings the day
   Effaces. A scarce broken calm
Broods o'er the scene, except the lay,
   That seems of gratitude a psalm,
Some fluttering tenant of the nest
Sings, ere she stills herself in rest.

The sighing of the rustling leaves
 Sounds like a whisper from a land
Where sin nor mars, nor sorrow grieves
 The breast.   We do not understand,
In our glad hours, why grim despair
For ever hangs upon the air.

Oh, in the unseen soul what hell
 May kill or blight its very day !
The jest, the laugh, may be the knell
 Of grief too great to ebb away :
Disease and pain the angel form
Rack, and its loveliness deform.

  *   *   *   *

He heedeth not the flight of time ;
 For, in the unforgotten past,—
That past that, distant, looms sublime,—
 He's girt in mem'ry's bondage fast,
And she is sitting by his side,
The maid who should have been his bride.

'Tis not, as some would have us think,
    Alone the future that allures
When hearts are sad ; it adds the link
    For those who hope for fame—assures
That ere few years have spun their round
The air with praises shall resound.

Unconsciously he lifts his gaze,
    When, motionless, an angel fair
Before him waits.   He silent prays
    For succour and the spirit's care ;
Reason once more returns to reign
Within his wild and weary brain.

The smiling past steals into view,
    The present also, with its dread ;
His soul from out the future drew
    What then as joy and love it read.
Ah, had he known the hand of Fate
Was soon to make all desolate !

Wise are all who value rightly
    The joys that spring within their reach—
Stars but pay their visits nightly,
    Between each day is there a breach :
And flow'rs, however bright their bloom,
Must wither—die,—for such their doom.

       *   *   *   *   *

"O angel bright !   Spirit eterne !
    I marvel not that thou should'st leave
The courts above, when thou didst learn
    Thy lovely counterpart did grieve.
To Esther is thy presence due ;
To comfort her this angel flew ! "

"Oscar, my own, no spirit I
    From other worlds ; not free from care
As angels are.   Fain would I fly
    (If thou could'st also come) to share
Their calm and downy rest—to dream
Beside some everlasting stream."

" Along this corridor I tread
   The weary hours of solemn night;
Where slumb'ring Nature, round me spread,
   Allays my sorrows, calms my sight;
The very starlets sympathise,
And call the tear-drops from mine eyes.

" Call from my heart, not from mine eyes !—
   My heart, my life—oh, death too slow !—
Ebbs, ebbs away in anguish'd sighs,
   An essence of the deepest woe.
My life is parcell'd into days
Of death, and each one ruthless slays.

" Ye stars !—ye gods !   There's nought but Fate,
   Blind chance—as many sadly deem ;
'Tis we ourselves a God create,
   Offspring of Hope's illusive dream ;
Or never wouldest thou have known
Such blasts as have upon thee blown."

" Oh, Oscar, thy wild sayings hush !
    Chance never made yon glorious dome !
So said I, in the earliest rush
    Of grief, till calmer thoughts came home.
Though little certain we may know,
Sometimes we feel a sacred glow,

" E'en if it be against our will—
    A deep pervading, living breath,
A something in the soul that still
    Will live when we are bow'd in death—
A voice that speaks—a voice that's dumb—
A foretaste of the life to come.

" We may not meet again, 'tis true,
    This is my guardians' stern decree ;
Sure reason they will find to rue
    Command which severs me from thee.
Thou art mine all, nor may'st thou stay—
This night we part, and part for aye.

" But once again to meet we were :
    To save mine honour and mine hand
This crushing oath I had to swear :
    Thro' life, till death, this is the band
That must encircle me ; no power
Can burst it, ere that solemn hour.

" So when the morning dawns we part.
    Oh, come not quick, thou morning light !
For when night breaks then breaks this heart,
    And when day dawns then comes my night,
That evermore will darker grow,
Till over me death's waters flow.

"A foreign prince of sounding name,
    Who kens the worth of gold and show,
Begg'd their consent that he might claim
    This hand and heart.   Lured by the glow
Of wealth, they vowed he soon should claim
Me for his bride.   Oh, sin and shame !

" To save mine honour thou hast heard
    The awful vow that must us part :
When night has sped no other word
    Must pass these lips, though bursts this heart.
This heart whose every beat is thine,
That rather dies than thee resign."

" Immortal Truth, why ours this gloom ?
    Nor would I grieve could I but bear
This weight of woe, this double doom
    Alone—my own and Esther's share.
I should not then have lived in vain,
Could I have shielded her from pain.

" Sweet love !   I haste where wild waves heave
    Their foaming crests aloft in air ;
Not that my grief I may relieve,
    But that its wildness I may bear.
Like storm-beat ship, we must ride on,
Though helm be lost and compass gone.

    *   *   *   *   *

" Afar I see the morning break,

    The dew 'gins glisten in its light,

A silver sheen now gilds the lake ;

    How soon the hours have wing'd their flight !

Our suns are set—and all we've left,

Are souls of all they love bereft.

" Another tress !   Though all are mine,

    It will recall the comely head

Whereon it hath been wont to shine

    In masses of pure golden thread ;

From out its gold those eyes of blue

In loveliness will e'er look through.

" To Fancy's eye there yet will be

    Those cherried lips with rose's bloom,

Teeth whiter than the foam of sea ;

    From out thy breast thy breath's perfume

Will waft its fragrance—bring to view

My all of hope—my Esther—you !"

" Oscar, the holy convent's near :
    Thither I'll haste to watch and pray,
To shed the sad repentant tear,
    My troubles on the altar lay ;
And at dark midnight vigils keep,
For God to guide thee o'er the deep.

" O hour too solemn e'en to weep—
    O soul too full to overflow—
O darkness than the grave more deep—
    O death than thee a deadlier blow—
Thy sickly hand but chills the clay,
But this my spirit seems to slay.

" And yet the time has come—Farewell !
    Upon my brain there rests a weight,
And in my soul there sounds a knell
    Than charnel-house more desolate—
Fierce anguish in mine ears doth ring,
The music of her iron string."

    *   *   *   *   *

Now clinging in a wild embrace,

    They kiss, they part, they kiss again ;

And in each feature you could trace

    Of that sad hour the bitter pain ;

For in their last and longing gaze

A fiery torment seem'd to blaze.

One last farewell ! He breaks away,

    And rushes wildly o'er the lawn ;

He knows that it were mad to stay,

    For now has fully broke the morn ;

But like a statue Esther stands,

With trembling heart, and clasped hands.

Her quiv'ring lips and brow of snow,

    Her blue and wildly-staring eye

From which the tear-drop will not flow,

    Her breast that heaves, yet gives no sigh,

Her cheeks once ruddy, now how pale,

Tell greater grief than any wail.

Yet from her lovely throat there broke
One cry of anguish so profound,
That every slumbering echo woke,
In response to that piercing sound.
Now on the turf she silent lies,
And dew-drops bathe her sightless eyes.

Yes, she is dead—or rather sleeps—
Her woes are hush'd, her heart is still;
She heeds not now that mourners weep
The damned deed they would fulfil.
Rough was her voyage—that voyage is o'er,
For her earth's billows roll not more.

*   *   *   *   *

But Oscar says that on the sea
She oft beside him seems to be,
And when on land thro' midnight gloom
He watches o'er her silent tomb :—

When the dew trembles on the grass,

And voiceless all the moments pass,

And heaven unfolds her mystic scroll,

And stars unnumber'd gem the pole,—

There's in the sadness of his eye,

The yearning of his pensive sigh,

His absent gaze, his bending form,

Heedless of solitude and storm,—

Something that tells how fain would he,

    Freed from the bonds that soul encumber,

Each fond regret of memory flee,

    And with his Love for ever slumber !

A DREAM.

I DREAM'D I floated on some river deep,
Whose course did wind a mighty forest
through ;
Far overhead burnt on the countless stars—
'Twas sad and silent, like to Death awoke !
Solemnity in awful stillness reign'd,
So calm and peaceful, like an old man's
prayer :
Noiseless, as if the wings of Sleep had lain
Upon that forest old—for when I spoke,
A whisper'd moan among the aged trees
I heard, which floated soon into the depth
Of the deep silence ; timidly afraid,
It was subdued like to a life in death.

Each ripple that did carry me, an age

Appear'd, and ere another ripple came,

Before my mind Eternity roll'd on :

So wond'rous and o'erwhelming in its flow,

The ages all were lost within its depth,

Engulf'd like mighty mountains 'neath its sea,

To rest with their forerunners, and to stand

Foundation for the æons yet to come.

Still gliding o'er this tideless river deep,

From out the forest, frosted o'er with age,

With visage calm and careworn did appear

A kindly man, whose pace bespoke his mood.

His feet did touch the earth caressingly,

As though it were a human form or friend

Whom he had loved and lost, and buried there.

Halting beneath a many-cent'ried tree,

He thus soliloquised : "Thou age-worn oak !

As mine, thy days are short and numbered :

Yea, thou that long hast rear'd aloft thy form,

That long hast held thy mighty head erect,

Must lay it 'neath the feet of conq'ring Time.

River ! oft floating in fantastic clouds

Beneath the sky—thou canst not say thou art

The same two moments long, for thou art not ;

Each sunbeam and each ebbing shaketh thee—

And no abiding place hath molecule ;

And these poor hoary locks are not the locks

Which cluster'd round my youthful brow; this
    ,   brow

All wrinkled, and so sorely mark'd with night,

Is not the same that burn'd with passion's
    heat.

Then wherefore am I old ? To-day I am

What yesterday I was not, and as young

As on my natal morn.   Oh, like this rush

Of water, chang'd, and yet the same—is Life !

And with few risings of the eastern sun,

These particles of flesh and brain that cling

So closely now, will mingle with the sands

Of some far desert land—and I no more !

Then will the atoms of this imag'ry

For ever be ?—while these wild thoughts must
    die—

This finer self that seems the echoing

" Of some deep voice we cannot comprehend :

This something which we love and awes us so,

Is all this then the magic tinkling note

Of centres of the brain ?—a magic thrill

Of some electric nerve?   'Tis hard to think,

And cruel to believe of Nature thus :

That she should labour and succeed so far,—

To crush and merge the individual life

With dull and senseless heaps of worthless mud.

She would be taking her own life, to keep

Herself from dying."

From out the old man's eyes there dropt a tear—

A tear made up of loneliness, despair,

And pity for the world at large—a tear

Half hope and half of sorrow, that his life

In searching had been spent, to find out

      nought—

A tear for fiery youth, that full of hope,

When he had passed away, should do as he—

Believing much at first, and having faith

Each day would teach them more—till, tired and

      faint,

D

They too should fall, with labour overspent,
With famish'd heart, and sorrow fathomless.
Still, by Life's current was I hurried on—
For ever on—absorbed in pensive thought,
When on mine ears was pour'd the plaintive
    voice
Of some fond love-sick youth, who on the turf
Was gazing at the pale, unfervid moon,
Whose light he pray'd to kiss his lady's brow,
And waken in her heart a dream of him.
With listless air upon the night he pour'd
Some tender sonnets, which his fever'd brain
Did feign believe would echo in her soul.
Poor youth ! so restless in expectancy,
Ere this, thou deemedst all thy weariness,
The hunger of thy soul, was want of love,
And now that restlessness by love is made
More constant and unsated than before.

Next came I, borne by the resistless tide,
To one upon whose stern-cut face there sate

Sincerity, as if 'twere interwove

With Hope, Doubt, Passion, and, alas! Despair.

For he had left the busy haunts of life,

And when I question'd him, he answer'd me:

" It is not that I hate my fellow-men;

I know not who or what they are—not one;

I see and hear, yet hear them not nor see—

Their words are only cover to their thoughts,

Their thoughts but obscurations of themselves.

It is this sham, yet semi-truthfulness,

It is the endless looking in the face

As if it were the individual,

This universal spirit of pretence,

That long has swept and sweeps so fast along;

That, ere another age has closed its eyes,

Man scarce will think of his diviner self,

But take his body for his whole estate;

So trustful is he in appearances,

And so accustomed to this varnishing,

He seldom recks it is a stolen gloss.

Oft I bethink me of mine earlier dreams,

Which then were mighty possibilities;

How, when I wander'd in the early light

That breaks so gently and so beautiful,

Like cheering ray from a sublimer world,

A spirit bright and mystical did sing,

And led me on as 'neath celestial spell;

The world was all aglow, and every sound

Was musical, and came direct from Heaven.

Now does life seem but a vast juggling game,

And he accounted best who keeps behind

The scenes, and throws the greatest light in
      front,

Though in his rear is nought but rising fumes,

As from some dark and loathsome charnel-
      house.

Nor does this surfacing belong to him

Of evil deeds alone. Men scarce will own

A gen'rous deed or thought, but feign to tell

'Twas not from kindly wish or impulse soft,

But some spasmodic action of the mind,

Or to have done with some importunate.

These latter ones forebode the deeper gloom.

There gleams some hope when man would hide

    his sin :

It speaks dissatisfaction in the wrong,

And discontent is father to a change ;

But woe is it when deeds are made less noble,

Because a man would blush to own him good—,

Yea, saddest woe to spoil a noble deed,

To hush an imputation that were just."

      *   *   *   *   *

All else I dream'd from memory hath 'scaped,

Save that at foot of some high-soaring peak,

Half buried, and dismemberèd, did lie

An image of the Goddess Poesy.

Wailing most bitterly this fiendish deed,

Did cluster close around her worshippers.

Anon I heard a scornful, mocking laugh,

Which came, I glean'd, from those who had

    destroy'd,

The people of these later days, who thirst

Alone for gold, upon whose brows is writ

A hungry, mammonistic selfishness.

Their eyes did anxious scan each brother man,

As if in horrid doubt of every one ;

With vulpine cunningness, all eager were

To clutch the gains of any one that gain'd.

From out the mourners of fair Poesy,

With flashing eyes and twitching, angry lips,

Stept one, to front this crowd of Mammonites.

He said, in voice of deepest irony :

" You tell me that, the Age of Poetry has gone !

Have, then, the lives of men grown musical of
        late ?

Does Concord reign, and universal Harmony ?

Has man at length learn'd his relationship with
        man,

That so on all their brows divine Contentment
        sits,

And therefore Peace ?　So Love's most musical
        of notes

Is struck from out the deepest heart—the darkest
  too—

And floats on every sunbeam'd breath which we
  inhale,

And thus the glorious, often foretold Age of
  Gold

Has come, to cool the too long heated lips of
  sin.

A World of Music! Music of a myriad souls—

The feeblest of them all in tune—"

I heard not more.

*   *   *   *   *

MUSINGS.

'Tıs night!   I stand alone in the wood,
The deep, dark wood ;
I have left the path the many tread
Few are the stars above my head,
And the owls are hooting shrill.
Shall I take the left, or take the right ?
Come to my aid, some fairy sprite,
And lead me on which way you will.
      In vain I call :
      I stumble and fall,
      Around my feet
      The briars do meet,
And ever my weary wanderings cheat.

I come to the river—'tis dark and cold,
Is there aught in its depths it will unfold?
I thrust in my hand and note its flow,
And think—what lies in its bed below;
Of the many floating idly along,
Who never have fought, but think themselves
      strong;
Of some who scarcely have ever thought,
Who take whatever they're told for truth,
And hurry along with the step of youth,
With strife of faith they never sought.
They look on me as a sinful man
On whose sad brow rests of Heaven the ban.
I answer nought—but I turn away,
And would, if I could, but I cannot pray,
Unless my doubts in this dreary night,
And these endless struggles after the light,
Is prayer—and I envy them not.

     *   *   *   *   *

Night has not passed, but 'tis nearing the morn,
I'm eagerly watching, weary and worn.
Dimly I see on the sands of old Time

Foot-prints of loveliness, goodness, and crime,

No longer distinct—interwoven and spun

In strangest of textures under the sun.

I dare not stand still, and there's danger
  ahead ;

Cut off from retreat, oh, which path shall I
  tread?

A messenger came in the form of a dove,

And bade me survey the far heavens above,

And follow the star most resplendent in light.

So thither I turn'd, where the dove came in sight :

Joy fill'd my heart, my fears were released,

I gazed on the star—'twas the Star of the East!

FLOWING, SMILING, E'ER BEGUILING.

FLOWING, smiling, e'er beguiling,
Like a pleasant, wayward maiden,
Runs life on.
Hearts that once were bright and cheery,
In the distance may grow weary;
Still Time's flood sweeps all along—
And the sorrows of the groaning,
Mixing with the sea's wild moaning,
But create a song.
All have moments of wild anguish,
When the brightest hopes must languish,
And we care not on to live.
Ah! we must not take *one* moment,
Nor the answer *it* would give—

Take the days, the months, or years;

All our joys, and all our tears;

Take the Winter with its wildness,

All the gloom it can unfold;

Then the Summer's radiant mildness,

And its roses bathed in gold;

In the twilight—and alone—

Peace calm sitting on her throne,

And there's nought to frighten Rest.

Gently slumb'ring on thy breast,

Take them all and o'er them muse—

This, nor that result, refuse;

Let pure reason lead the way,

Nor let illusive Fancy play.

Having made a calm decision,

With right judgment, and precision,

Look ye upwards to the skies,

Know that there your journey lies,

Thankfully your pathway tread.

Though your feet be on the dead,

Is not bright Heaven overhead?

I LOVE TO DREAM.

DREAMS! Dreams! I love to dream the golden
    hours away,
In some quiet bower, in a lonely hour, to let my
    fancy play,
To be all alone when the birds have flown, and
    the sky wears a crimson blush :
How sweet to note, as the zephyrs float, night's sweet
    and solemn hush !
To think of days, so young and bright, so free from
    doubt's alloy,
When hearts were warm and fill'd with light—and a
    little maiden coy—
And I love to feel again so sad, as sad and lonely
    too,

As when the clouds first gloom'd o'erhead, and
young hope frighten'd flew.

Oh, my heart doth heave, and I feel as sad, as sad
and as solemn too,

As I did when first the night came on, and its
curtains closely drew.

And now of life I know not more, though burning
thoughts I've had—

I know not if joy or tears be best, or whether I am
mad;

I only know my faith is less than when I was a
child,

I only know the soul within is darker and more
wild.

This grand old world and all it holds, I feel and
know I love,

Nor do these eyes by faith e'en see a fairer world
above,

And yet within so strange, so deep, a voice I often
hear—

A voice so far, so mystical, that bids me vainly
cheer:

For *I only know* I love to dream the golden hours
  away,

In quiet bower, in lonely hour, to let my fancy play,

To be all alone when the birds have flown, and the
  sky wears a crimson blush,

To silent note, as the zephyrs float, night's sweet and
  solemn hush.

TO THE MUSE.

Sweet Goddess ! Soul of pure and living fire !
For thee I claim great Orpheus as sire.
Art not the echo of the golden strings
From which divinest harmony he flings,
That on the balmy air Elysian floats,
And charms Olympus with the magic notes?
Sweet essence of the melody of life,
Divinest concord in this world of strife,
Whose horrid discords, wide contrasting, make
Thy voice in richer purity to wake,
Breathe in my soul thy deep prophetic word,
That, when I sing, my tuneful voice be heard.

Or must the dreams that long have fed this
    soul,
Returning there, with curses o'er it roll?
Then Disappointment, drive thy heavy car
Till I am ground beneath its wheels; not far
Ahead the time, perchance, when rage shall rise
Within my breast and storm against the skies.
'Tis true that I have borne and still can bear—
The heart that has been torn, fate still may tear—
And yet I weep to think how harsh the strain
From my poor lute will be when born of pain.
Must I, who always felt a kind desire
To wake but happy music from my lyre,
Light my poor lines at Anger's fitful flame,
And by upbraiding Fate my wrath proclaim?
Sweet months of dreams so bright, a sad fare-
    well!
Within my soul I note thy passing knell.
Oh, were it but the knell of doubt and fear,
And heralding of brighter days I hear!
E'en though ye're false, sweet hopes, we must
    not part,

E

For ever breathe within this lonely heart.

With you to bless, and throw a cheering ray,

My barque may glide along its devious way,

Till o'er Death's ocean, wild and wide, my
    view

May catch the gleam of Life's immortal hue.

Had I not loved—this song were glad and
    sweet—

Had she not joy'd, with love, that love to greet.

Ah, Disappointment, whelm this struggling soul,

So over hers thy billows do not roll !

She is too gentle, modest, and too fair,

For thee to touch the ringlets of her hair.

Thy pitiless hand nigh nipp'd her in the
    bloom,

When 'cross her early path the ghastly tomb

Its shadows deep and long in sadness flung,

And almost from her heart the life-blood
    wrung.

So haste thee, Demon ! or the Poet's verse

Shall stand to damn thee with a living curse.

E'en with contentment would I lay mine head

With those that sleep the slumber of the
    dead.
Nor do I weep to think this voice were hush'd,
Or hand that writes were mingled with the
    dust,
And that I never heard a breath of Fame
Proclaim to some poor few my humble name,
Were it not that I loved; for I am young,
And Nature will not from her throne be flung.
I sigh not to be free, the sweetest note
To mortals known has from this soul awoke;
I sigh that sadden'd Hope and unreap'd Trust
Do thro' my brain their burning arrows thrust;
My mind, long tortured with a searching fire,
Trembles with strength of long-suppress'd
    desire—
Desire of life, of thought unfetter'd, free
To see the round of life's reality.

    Must I, whose soul would swell with
    ecstasy
The sleeping lakes and heaving waves to see;

I, who should stand aghast, and feel a God,
Where mountains lift their heads—where men
    have trod,
Renown'd for greatness, who have left behind
Strange links that to the past the present
    bind,
Live chain'd to one dull, unenchanted spot,
By all save Hope and Discontent forgot?
For Hope, e'er riding on her fiery steed,
The downfalls of the past will little heed,
But paints the future with a richer glow,
As rougher now the adverse winds do blow.
Oh, could I only give my fancy wing,
To follow Nature where her voices ring !
My lowly verse, unfetter'd from its dread,
Should soar aloft with glory-crownèd head—
And, ever seeking to be pure and bright,
Should point men onwards to the realms of
    light.
For on the Natal Day its strains should rise,
And claim the new-born blessings from the
    skies,—

A happy childhood, freed from sorrow's tears ;

A youth that trustful look'd for manhood's
years ;

A manhood brave, victorious in the fight;

A soul for ever striving for the right.

Its voice the sprightly village youths should
cheer,

And bid depart the love-lorn maiden's tear.

When evening threw its twilight o'er the vale,

They'd list with gladness to its thrilling tale ;

With hand in hand in silence should they
woo,

Each deeper loving as they closer drew,

And pressing shyly to each other's breast,

Should find a true and often sigh'd-for rest :

And vowing love, should seal it with a kiss,

Dreaming that ever after life was bliss.

But on the sacred, happy Nuptial Day,

My song should breathe its most ethereal lay,

Prosperity and peace, a home of love,

And every blessing from the gods above,

Serener happiness and deeper trust—

As years should wed past years, in order just.
Kind mothers, yearning for their children dead,
Should round their graves with lighter footsteps
    tread ;
The aged, gazing on the setting sun,
Should ponder on their own race, nearly run,
And smiling hopeful on the crimson sky,
On life's long day look back, resign'd to die.

ART THOU IN THE DESERT?

AND is it in the desert that thou art?
  So lonely and unfriended dost thou feel?
And do fierce tempests dash against thine heart,
  And make thy soul in very doubt to reel?

And is it in the wilderness, athirst,
  Thou wanderest, unhoused and hungry too?
On memory do smiling rivers burst,
  Yet now thou canst not taste the morning dew.

Be brave ! Fear not the tempter's power, but pray,
  And think of Him, thy Saviour, gone before;
Put all thy trust in Him who is the Way,
  And to the Throne of God the only Door.

Though sick and faint, though maim'd thy
    weary feet,
    Thou still art near His home, and should'st
        thou fall,
'Twill only be thy gracious Lord to meet,
    To sit beside Him in his Banquet Hall.

A few more struggles in the desert sand,
    A few more hopes and fears and sorrows here,
And thou shalt clasp the guiding, loving Hand
    That from thine eyes shall wipe each burning
        tear.

.

A GRAVE SCENE.

Yon gentle mother, young and fair,
  Stoops o'er her darling's mound ;
Her heart beats sadly to and fro,
  Her gaze is on the ground.

She peers right through the solid earth,
  And sees her own sweet child
In all the beauty of its health,
  Ere 'twas by death defiled.

She feels it folded to her breast,
  She hears its pretty talk—
The gentle patter of its feet
  Adown the garden walk.

She's leaning on the marble slab,
　　And weeping o'er the sod,
Her spirit breaks away and flies
　　To heaven and to its God.

They found her lying on the grave,
　　All pale, and cold, and dead.
They laid her with her child to rest,
　　In Nature's quiet bed.

ON A FADED LEAF.

O NLY a faded leaf that flits away;

Yet, wither'd leaf, thou hast a word to say

To him who humbly, reverently seeks

The awful lessons mighty Nature speaks.

Leaf! thou hast had thy spring, thy summer too,

And thou hast lost thy crimson golden
hue;

No more thou gleamest, dancing in the
sun,

For now thy dreary winter hath begun.

Yes, thou hast had thy seasons; now decay

Will all thy tender fibres waste away.

Like thee, sad monitor, we're fading too,

Some e'en before they've donn'd life's

summer hue,

And, though we autumn reach or winter

see,

Wither'd we fall at last from off the living

tree.

MY TRUE LOVE IS DEAD!

Roses all ruddy and gay,
Why are ye blooming so brightly to-day ?
　　Droop low each proud head;
　　　Each petal let fall,
　　　Sadly, silently all,—
　　My true Love is dead !

Bird on the blithesome wing,
Why a carol of joy this day dost thou sing ?
　　Breathe a sad dirge instead;
　　　As thou mountest on high
　　　In the blue fields of sky—
　　My true Love is dead !

Brooklet, rushing along,
Why mid the sedges that jubilant song ?
Be still in thy bed ;
Or thy note change to woe
As thy waves onward flow,—
My true Love is dead ?

Roses, droop ye no more ;
Sweet bird, I pray thee, thy song give not o'er ,
Smile, brook, in thy bed ;
For a voice sweet and low,
Bids me not weep, although—
My true Love be dead !

A MOTHERLESS MAID.

THE sun shot his last bright beam o'er the
    sky,
Her young, weary breast breathed forth a deep
    sigh ;
Down came the snow-flakes that kiss'd her
    soft cheek—
Poor little maiden, so modest and meek.
Sadly and lonely she plodded along,
The chill winds whistled a mystical song ;
All alone on the moor, in darkness and night,
Journey'd, unfriended, this poor little wight.
Deep fell the shadows as onward she flew,
Keener and stronger the northern winds blew,

Pale was her face, in each eye stood a tear—
Hungry ! with nothing to feed on but fear.
In the wide world had she never a home,
Nought for a shelter save heaven's high dome.

Hark ! There is music !—and, yes, there's a
    light !
See, thro' the windows, how happy and bright
Those young faces are by the glow of the fire,
All things around them their hearts can desire.
" Ah !" sigh'd the maiden, " how strange to
    forget,
'Tis to welcome old Christmas those children
    have met;
Were mother now living, oh, then should I be
Happy and joyous as those that I see !
Hush ! 'Twas surely her voice in the gloom
    that I heard !—
Ah, no ! 'tis the note of some wandering bird ;
How could I fancy my mother was here,
Since she left me for heaven, 'tis a wearisome
    year ? "

Pale little maiden, alone in the snow,
Soon wilt thou be with her spirit, I trow.

Motherless child, thy cold pillow is white,
And it seems to sweet slumber thy soul to
    invite.
Art thou so drowsy ?—then sleep, my child,
    sleep !
Over thy pillow is no one to weep ;
And doth the glad music that falls on thine ear
Even thy poor little lonely heart cheer ?
Oh ! how canst thou smile ?—what fills thee with
    light ?
Is thy soul in sweet ecstasy ready for flight ?
Or dost thou fancy thou hearest the tread
Of feet that are silent around thy cold bed ?

Flees the dark night, driven out by the day—
Out rush the children, all eager for play ;
What is it lying so white and so chill ?
Hands that for ever from hence must be still.

F

Kiss that cold brow, ere it rests in the grave ;

Kiss that calm cheek, it belong'd to the brave ;

Find her a bed near the yew-tree's deep shade,

And say that here lieth a " motherless maid " !

FLUSH, CHEEK AND BROW.

Flush, cheek and brow, and flash, dull eye ;
And kindle, heart, to glowing heat ;
May every breath bring forth a sigh,
Till brain shall madden in its seat,
And all my wishes be to die.

Few, few have dream'd of nobler things
Than I in years that now have sped ;
Oh, that I too were blest with wings !
How few the hours till I were fled !
I'd rather know the worst death brings,

Than, wrapt in clouds, see streaks of light
That haunt like fascinating dreams,
Which, soon as Fancy fails, take flight,
Leaving unnavigable streams,
'Neath canopy as dark as night.

Oh, who has yearn'd as I have yearn'd,
To read the complex scroll of life?
Thro' silent nights my soul hath burn'd
To find some order in its strife—
But little certain I discern'd.

In Nature, who but oft hath heard,
Or dream'd he heard, a voice divine?
From rustling leaves to song of bird,
One fain would trace some deep design,
Or care of God on man conferr d.

But when, or where, or how, by whom?
Now halts the beat of Hope's bright wing,
And boundless thought is cramp'd for room,
And can but work within a ring,
Or seek for life while in a tomb.

'Tis hard to break from all the dreams
That youth so fondly dreamt were true;
'Tis hard to stay those smiling streams,
Whose course our earliest fancies drew,
And o'er us flung their sparkling beams.

Oft have I gazed, on starry night,
Upon those silent, distant worlds,
Till in my soul hath glow'd a light,
And Doubt from off his throne been hurl'd,
And Faith has fill'd my soul with sight.

'Tis Faith at which I fall.   A lie,

However great, a truth is still,

To him who does it thus descry.

Where he undoubting takes his fill,

Do counter roads lead to the sky?

WHEN PASSION DOTH, &c.

WHEN passion doth my temples heat,
And curses rise within my soul,
Thy farewell smile, so sad and sweet,
Doth like a Lethe o'er them roll.

When driven mad with wild despair,
When hope and doubt together clash,
When I would fling away all care,
Thy winning smile doth round me flash,

And keeps me wrapt in thoughts of thee.
Thy soft, sweet voice on echo's wing
Doth thrill my soul with ecstasy,
And hopes of brighter times doth bring.

Then calmer, I can meet my fate,
And work, work on, though fill'd with fear,
Till with that work I grow elate,
And see thee smiling—feel thee near.

The battle's won ! I hear my name,
And claim thine hand (for heart is mine),
And, stepping onwards into fame,
Rejoice the most it made me thine.

So, trusting maiden, smile, smile on :
Dreams are the mothers of great things.
The fairest bird could never fly
If pruned were its airy wings.

So smiling, smile, till death be ours,
Nor murmur, though our dreams prove vain.
'Tis much thou hast made radiant hours,
That otherwise had brought me pain.

MY SOUL, GREAT GOD.

My soul, great God, doth turn to Thee,
 Breathing a timid, doleful dirge,
 Quiv'ring fearful on the verge
Of that unknown which is to be.

Wondering within itself it lives ;
 For ever yearns for scenes more fair,
 And droops o'er-burdened with care,
Killing itself by what it gives.

Sadness, with hue of deepest dye
 Obscures the dark, mysterious past,
 Nor can my mind the future cast ;
'Tis blacker still.   I know not why

The past seems lost, the present waste,
        I know not what I fain would be !
        For, like a ship adrift at sea,
I know not to what port I haste.

Why do my temples ache with thought ?
        Why do my soul such thoughts appal ?
        'Tis said Thou seest a sparrow fall,
Thou canst not count me then as nought.

Oh, Thou art God ! Enough for me
        The strength Thou givest day by day.
        Hush my complaints, and lead the way
To that long home—Eternity !

TO DEATH.

THOU at whom the bravest tremble,
Tell what most thou dost resemble?
Hast thou any shape, or being,
Art thou blind, or all things seeing?

Dost thou gaze with wild grimaces,
When we're dying, in our faces?
Dost thou gibber,—madly howl,—
From out the shadow of some cowl?

Art thou quick, or art thou ling'ring,
Feel we thee our vitals fing'ring?
Or art thou but a thought, a dream
In which eternity doth gleam?

Ah, death ! thy hand but breaks the thread
That binds our souls—not ought to dread.
Yet whisper, do our spirits rise
At once, and scale the distant skies?

Ah, yes ! they do not beat dismay'd,
On heavenly air their wings are laid,
Called by the God who gave them,
For His Son hath died to save them.

WE DID NOT KISS.

WE did not kiss, we could not sigh,
Nor murmur e'en a faint good-bye,
For there breathed a holy feeling,
Round our hearts a holy feeling.
In that first and silent gazing
Was a gladness, deep, amazing.
We needed not our lips to open,
For a wondrous love was spoken
In that strange and sudden spell,
And the dreamy, mute farewell,
In that hand which press'd so slightly,
In those fingers gliding lightly
'Neath the cover of mine own,
Like weary bird to shelter flown.

Thus we met, and thus we parted,
Thus a wondrous hope was started,
'Neath whose blending, magic sway
Roll'd six seasons fast away.
Once again these hasting feet
Guide me my fair love to meet.
See, again her heart's blood rushing,
Paints its richness in a blushing;
Silent are our lips as ever,
Lingeringly our fingers sever.
From our eyes a light is streaming,
Bright and loving, and we're dreaming,
Do not speak, we are but dreaming.

Oft we've met, and oft we've spoken,
Vows have utter'd, nor have broken.
Ah! I will not say how often
I have kiss'd that truthful brow,
Only tell you it is often,
Every kiss a solemn vow.
And within her soul is yearning
With a bright, immortal burning

Of true love's o'erwhelming light.
Yea, her love is infinite.
See how wild my future gladness,
How serenely stalketh sadness;
Wrapt in such a cloak of sweetness,
Darkest hours must pass with fleetness.
Maddest anguish will assail me,
Nought on all the earth avail me,
Should stern sorrow leave his traces
On that best of angel faces.
Yet how nobly would she meet him?
Bravely, like a woman, greet him,
Stemming all the dark and danger,
Till life's rest should come ;
And the Babe of Bethlehem's manger
Call'd her spirit home.

I SAW LAST NIGHT.

I SAW last night the new-born shining moon,
Then whisper'd thought with onward gaze how soon
Into its fullest grandeur it would grow,
And on a darken'd world its radiance throw.

At early morn I view'd the glorious sun.
Oh! it was from my left; he had begun
To run his daily race, and I thought too
That from my left another sun ('twas you)

Did rise, to be the brightness of my days,
By shedding on their sadness, gentle rays
Of love and hope—immortal rays of light,
That darkness for an instant could not blight.

And then, great hopes of that which happen may
Pass'd thro' my mind with meteoric ray,
And rent the heavy veil of time unborn,
Which fancy painted like a smiling morn.

Then far away I saw a tapering spire,
Which, steep'd in golden sun, shone like a fire,
Reminding me of beacon lights of yore
That lit up Britain's isle from shore to shore.

I thought that spire a beacon was to me,
For 'neath its shadow we might wedded be.
Just then the sun behind a cloud did pass,
And now thou shin'st for me no more, alas !

ONE SO DARK AND ONE SO FAIR.

One so dark and one so fair,
Each as beautifully rare
As southern days in northern climes—
And with souls as pure and white
As snow on sunny Alpine height,
Their voices like cathedral chimes.

One has eyes of heavenly blue—
For heaven alone can match their hue—
With a depth as soft and clear
As the moon when she doth take
Her rest upon some limpid lake,
The traveller's wanderings to cheer.

Ah, beneath those dreamy eyes
Many a hidden fountain lies,
All too ready to burst forth !
For if aught should cloud their sun,
Down the sparkling crystals run,
Born of gentleness, not wrath.

Oh, she is too rare and fair
Half the ills of life to bear—
Too sensitive and finely spun ;
A maid alone for smiling hours,
For gentle winds and sweetest flow'rs,
Or home beneath the southern sun.

But I loved her, and 'twas sweet
To sit whisp'ring at her feet,
And, if life were free from sorrow,
A meet companion she would be
To sail upon its laughing sea,
And smiling greet each glad to-morrow.

Sages tell it is not so,
Joy is intermix'd with woe.
Then to her with locks of thunder,
From whose eyes the lightning flashes,
Driven by their silken lashes
That are quivering as with wonder,

Will I hasten.   Note her face,
Its infinitude of grace ;
Those lips of love ; that glance so true
Sympathetically stole
To the sadness of my soul,
And its deep-rankling barb outdrew.

Ah, when anguish wrings my heart
Comes this maid to share the smart,
Murm'ring not that doleful sorrow
Mingles with all earthly pleasures—
Pressing onwards to those treasures
Death will grant us on some morrow.

MOST LOVELY GIRL.

Most lovely girl ! Most gentle maid !
Thy loveliness hath flung a shade
Around all earthly forms, so dark,
They seem to thy great light a spark.

Ah, gentle maid ! I fain would tell
Its radiancy hath thrown a spell
About my heart, hath changed my lot,
Hath turn'd to heaven an earthly spot.

Old Time may part us in his flight,
Thy blooming beauty he may blight,
But ne'er on memory's page efface
Of thy sweet form the lovely trace.

Thy eyes, their light, their depth of love
Might draw a spirit from above,
So marvel not that I should be
So fervently in love with thee.

Where'er I be, whate'er my fate,
'Tis thou wilt be its potentate ;
The years may come, the years may go,
Still I am thine thro' weal and woe.

Oh, that thine heart might beat for me !
I only live that day to see.
I wish indeed the time were gone,
That is, before we two are one.

Most lovely maid !　I fain would tell
How thought of thee doth throw a spell
About my heart, doth bless my lot,
Doth turn to heaven an earthly spot.

THE SWALLOWS.

Lo ! The swallows return
    All happy and free ;
And leave with its moaning
    The wild, angry sea.
The sunshine hath call'd them
    From lands far away,
They hasten to answer
    With little delay.
When summer has left us,
    They also will flee,
And with them their young ones,
    Far o'er the wild sea ;
For they could not endure
    The frost and the snow,
So they seek a new home
    Where the warm zephyrs blow.

And have we not often,
　　When friends have grown chill,
Wish'd wings that would find us
　　Warm hearts at our will?
Ah, could we by wishing
　　Our spirits set free,
And send them forth wandering
　　O'er life's changeful sea!
Ah, then, pretty swallows,
　　Where, where should we go?
We'd haste to life's sunshine,
　　And flee from its snow!

LITTLE BIRDIE, WHY SO GAY?

LITTLE birdie, why so gay,
Dancing on the leafless spray?
Thou art happy!   Then let me
Also, birdie, happy be.

Spring and summer have gone by;
Autumn also soon must die;
Winter, birdie, soon will be
Sweeping o'er the land and sea.

Dost thou, songster, know its chill
May thy stirring notes make still?
Cold and hunger, little friend,
May thy thread of life soon rend.

Nobly dost thou meet thy fate !
Dancing, singing, all elate—
Thou wilt warble while 'tis light,
Though thou perish in the night.

Why am I less glad than thou ?
Why sits sorrow on my brow?
Thou art happy !   Then let me
Also, birdie, happy be !

FADED BUNCH OF VIOLETS.

Faded bunch of violets,
  Thy fragrance now has fled ;
Crystal dew no longer swells
  Each tiny petal head.

Pretty bunch of violets,
  I knew not thou wert here,
And ye know not, poor flow'rets,
  Your presence calls a tear.

Ah, more than that thou callest !
  The lovely raven hair,
When thou wert blooming brightest,
  She partly hid thee there.

Oh, wert *thou only* faded !
  Oh, wert *thou only* dead !
Alas, that maiden dearest
  Has droop'd her darling head.

Before to earth they bore her,
  Upon her chilly breast
A bunch of thy companions
  With trembling hands I press'd.

Yes, she has gone, and darkness
  Has since surrounded me,
And yet in this I'm happy:
  Is not my darling free ?

She, poor wither'd violets,
  Has long since lost her bloom,
And o'er her angel features
  Hath closed the silent tomb.

Ah, *thou* art past recalling !
Thy beauty all has fled,
But everlasting springtide
Encircles her sweet head.

SLEEP ON, SWEET LOVE.

Sleep on, sweet love, the moon shines bright,
The stars sing silent over thee,
And Philomel awakes the night
With songs to thy dear memory.

Her notes have been more wild of late,
And seem to pierce yon distant sky;
Ah, maiden mine, she weeps thy fate,
And fain would reach thine ear on high!

Pause, Philomel! That song's thy soul.
Ah, now thou seest her lonely grave!
Live, nightingale, and round it troll
Thro' the dark hours some solemn stave.

Sleep, purest one, for I am near,
And o'er thy breast the grass is green ;
Adown each blade the dewy tear
Doth weep for thy return, I ween.

Sleep on, thou art not all alone,
Sweet thoughts and prayers are ever here ;
The unwearying winds around me moan,
Oft sorrow drops a burning tear.

Dream on, dream on, the moon shines bright,
The stars sing silent over thee,
And Philomel awakes the night
With songs to thy dear memory.

TO MY MOTHER ON HER JUBILEE.

ARISE with might, most holy Muse,
    And kindle in mine heart thy fire;
In every worthy thought infuse
    The gracious influence of thy lyre.

Ye grasses green, ye ferns and flow'rs,
    Burst ye forth in glorious gladness,
Come, add new pleasures to the hours,
    And banish every sadness.

Let Nature sing in one great song,
    The sea-waves dance more merrily;
Oh, may no shadows roll along,
    But all be brightness verily.

Sing, birds, with sweeter note your lays,
　　Sing, all ye good on land or sea ;
Make this the happiest of days,
　　For 'tis my mother's jubilee.

And every one that knoweth her,
　　As well as friends, as well as we,
Will breathe a wish, will say a prayer,
　　Who hear it is her jubilee.

And all will hope the future years
　　May ever bright and happy be,
Making amends for past arrears,
　　Crowning with joy thy jubilee !

May all be light, may all be smiles !
　　May nought but love still live with thee !
May glory fill the time that wiles
　　Us further from thy jubilee.

H

How many years we hope to spend,
　　How many years we trust to see,
When joy your smile will help to lend,
　　As ere thy day of jubilee !

May every wish of every day
　　Be granted now in love to thee ;
May time more happy flee away,
　　Since thou hast seen thy jubilee.

May heaven itself grow brighter far,
　　And may thy vision clearer see
The guidance of the morning star,
　　When thou hast pass'd thy jubilee.

I SORROW FOR THEE
THIS MORN.

I SORROW for thee this morn, my love!
    For thine heart is sad and lone,
And yearns for one who to realms above
    Two sad, long years hath flown.

Thy soul will crave for the past to-day,
    And anguish will wring thy breast;
Thou'lt live with him who glided away
    To an everlasting rest.

He knoweth thy weariness and grief,
    And sees how true is that heart;
He'll pray an angel bring thee relief,
    And strength to thy soul impart.

Yea, passing sweet was that father's love,
  And though long since call'd away,
He thinks on thee still in realms above,
  Where love has an endless day.

I know you would not wish to recall
  Him back to this world of strife,
Where friendships pass, and ills must befall,
  And sorrow and death are rife.

Think of him now, and not of his past,
  He lives in the realms of light;
Here *every* day must be overcast,
  Above it is *ever* bright.

Weep not thy loss, rather joy in his gain,
  Look upwards for strength to bear ;
Trust and hope some day to meet again,
  In the saintly city so fair.

I sorrow for thee to-day, my love !
    For thine heart is sad and lone,
Yearning for one who to realms above
    Two sad, long years hath flown.

FATHER CHRISTMAS.

Do I hear thee, Father Christmas, on the crisping
    snow?
From thy breathing comes the sighing, when the chill
    winds blow.
Is it from thy rosy cheeks the red sun steals his
    glow?
Be not timid, frosty parent, we have waited thee,
And our right hands, far extended, welcome heartily!
Come and set thee in our centre, sparkle in our
    bowl,
Though thy hands are iced over, warm thy genial
    soul;
Let its fervour, deeper glowing, over all hearts
    roll;
From our midst drive all dissension, let no face be
    sad.

Though our past has been but mournful, let us now
  be glad.
Are we fearful of the future, looms it then so
  dark?
Gently raise our drooping spirits, light Hope's
  cheering spark,
Let us have to bear us onwards Trust's auspicious
  barque.
Come, thou guest of many winters, don thy gayest
  robe,
Till good wishes further rolling circle all the globe.
Leave us many a kind remembrance, so the coming
  year
In its retrospective glances may find much to cheer.
So we'll haste to hear thee, father, on the crisping
  snow,
Knowing from thy rosy cheeks the red sun steals his
  glow.

SINCE THOU ART ALL MY OWN, FAIRY.

Why do I feel this dread,
And dream of breakers ahead,
Since thou art all my own, Fairy ?

Why should I fear to try
The tone of the critic's cry,
Since thou art all my own, Fairy?

'Tis because were I to meet
From fortune a defeat,
Thou would'st feel it too, Fairy.

Then those sweet eyes of blue
Would sting me (so bright and true)
If I couldn't make you mine, Fairy.

Yet I will flee this dread,
These dreams of breakers ahead,
And dream of thee instead, Fairy.

HER LOOK WHEN LAST.

HER look when last we had to part,
Unto my sad and weary heart
Said more than any words could say,
Or any happy minstrel's lay.

Her deep, dark eyes so full of light,
Shot thro' my soul and banish'd night,
A ray of hope they set on fire,
And struck my love's long-silent lyre.

They told me more than she would tell,
They told me that she loved me well.
Oh ! that last look, where'er I be,
Seems resting solemnly on me.

Oh, beauteous girl ! all life's dark day
Bestow that look, and light my way,
For thy sad gaze would e'er impart
A " sacred halo " round my heart.

ALL WILL YET COME RIGHT.

ANGELS sing with lips attuned,
That with us on earth communed,
"All will yet come right!"

Angels clothed in shining white,
Whisper thro' our darken'd night,
"All will yet come right!"

Angels in that happy clime,
Whisper down our fleeting time,
"All will yet come right!"

Angels by the Pearly Gate,
Sing a song with joy elate,
    "All will yet come right!"

Angels in the Streets of Gold,
Tell that tale, the sweetest told,
    "All will yet come right!"

Angels on the Crystal Sea,
Breathe it sweetly now to me,
    "All will yet come right!"

Angels by the King of Kings,
Sing the song with folded wings,
    "All will yet come right!"

Angels in the Heavenly Choirs,
Strike it forth from all their lyres,
    "All will yet come right."

Angels, sing with Seraphim,

Choruss'd by the Cherubim,

" All will yet come right."

WYMAN AND SONS, PRINTERS, GREAT QUEEN STREET, LONDON, W.C

www.ingramcontent.com/pod-product-compliance
Lightning Source LLC
Chambersburg PA
CBHW032101010726
47493CB00008B/2485